In honor of the Divine and the divinely female: to the
storm of stars I know as my mother, Ruthie; grandmothers;
sister-friends; and womanly wonders who taught me all
that we can be. Shine on. —B. B.

To my younger self. —T. F.

Text copyright © 2022 by Brynne Barnes.
Illustrations copyright © 2022 by Tatyana Fazlalizadeh.

Library of Congress Cataloging-in-Publication Data available.

ISBN 978-1-4521-6487-8

Manufactured in China.

Design by Jennifer Tolo Pierce.
Typeset in Begum and Limes Sans.
The illustrations in this book were rendered in oil
and acrylic paint on gesso board.

10 9 8 7 6 5 4 3 2 1

Chronicle Books LLC
680 Second Street
San Francisco, California 94107

Chronicle Books—we see things differently. Become part
of our community at www.chroniclekids.com.

BLACK GIRL RISING

by Brynne Barnes

illustrations by Tatyana Fazlalizadeh

chronicle books · san francisco

Who told you to twirl, Black girl,

like curls in your hair?

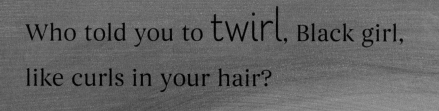

Who told you to skip, Black girl,

like sparrows in air?

Now don't you dare climb, climb, climb

Langston's crystal stair.

You ain't gonna make it, girl.

Come, get down from there.

Who are you to rise, Black girl,

like Angelou say?

You ain't no sun, Black, Black girl.

Put that shine away.

No one told you to be so strong
for all the world to see.

No one told you to be a girl,
a Black girl, just like me.

Who do you think you are now, girl—
a song that Nikki spins?
Made soft and Black and beautiful
from bass to trebled grin.

Ain't polite to recite rainbows,
head held high in their face.
You'd better keep quiet; keep still.
So you can know your place.

You ain't supposed to love, girl—

you or no one else.

You're supposed to run and hide.

Go. Hide from yourself—

from your skin, your lips, your freckles, your fade,

your fro, your naps, your dreads, your braids,

your blowout, your kinks, your twists, your waves,

your coils, so free and unafraid.

Who gave you that crown so wonderfully made?

You're supposed to dim your light

and never be seen.

But you don't, girl—you won't, girl—
you know you're a queen.

Electric butterfly,
you are more than you seem,
more than they talk,
a dangerous dream.

You are a thousand CUrlS unfurling in your hair.

You are a thousand fiStS standing proudly in air.

You are the SONG of swallows, lifting sun as they sing—

breaking light with their beaks,

breaking sky with their wings.

You're symphonies of fire.

In your wake, we're consumed.

There's chorus in your charisma,

a Black ballad in bloom—

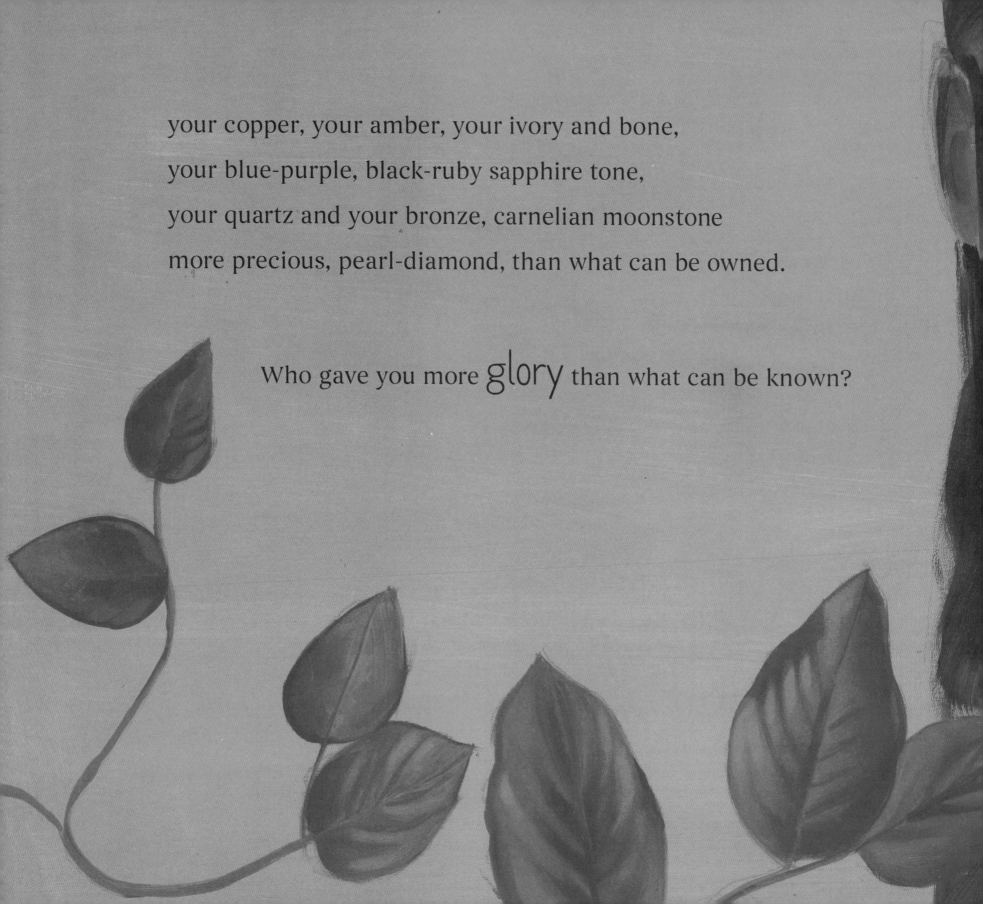

your copper, your amber, your ivory and bone,

your blue-purple, black-ruby sapphire tone,

your quartz and your bronze, carnelian moonstone

more precious, pearl-diamond, than what can be owned.

Who gave you more glory than what can be known?

You are the wish and the word,
the voice and the muse.
You're the melody rising,
the bliss of the blues.

You are Toni's good fortune,
Rita's lady freedom tune.
You are Mari's black cypress.
You are Gwendolyn's Jazz June.

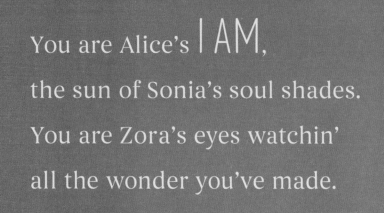

You are Alice's I AM,

the sun of Sonia's soul shades.

You are Zora's eyes watchin'

all the wonder you've made.

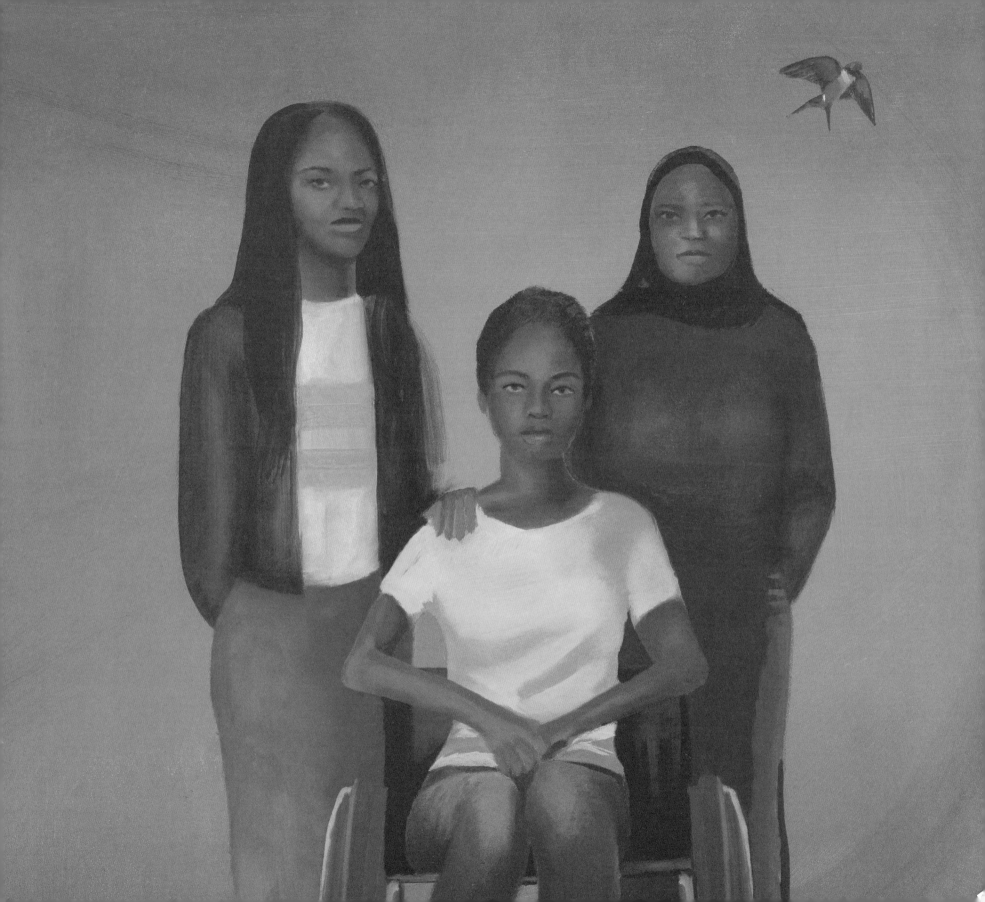

What's to come, wonderful one,

is in the crease of your hand;

it's in the **might** of your step,

everywhere your new light lands.

Shake off your ashes, girl,

    crack open the stark night.

This **new day** is yours to make, to take, girl.

    Take wing—

and ignite.